Lighthouse Letters

Annabelle Crystal

Contents

Introduction

In the quaint coastal town where the sea whispers secrets to those who listen, where every sunrise paints a new day's promise on the canvas of the horizon, lives Lena, a woman whose soul is as deep and vast as the ocean she adores. Her life, marked by routine and comfort, is intricately woven into the fabric of this close-knit community. It is a life she loves and one she has never thought to question, until a chance virtual encounter with Alex, a celebrated but solitary author, introduces her to an unexpected tide of emotion.

From their first email exchange, the connection between Lena and Alex is palpable, a meeting of minds and souls that neither expected but both desperately needed. It's a connection that asks them both to reconsider what they thought their futures held. It asks them to be brave. Through heartfelt conversations that span miles and breach the deepest corners of their guarded hearts, they nurture a bond as profound as it is complicated.

But the path of true love, as it often does, winds through a thicket of uncertainty and fear. For Alex, the solitude it demands has dedicated whose life to his craft and shaped, the thought of intertwining his world with Lena's, of venturing into the unknown territory of life as part of a pair, is both intoxicating and terrifying. For Lena, who carries the heartbeat of her coastal town within her, embracing this burgeoning love means risking the comfortable life she cherishes.

It is within this delicate dance, between love and fear, between holding on and letting go, that our story unfolds. With the quaint coastal town and its endearing residents as the backdrop, we journey with Lena and Alex as they navigate the nuanced symphony of falling deeply, irrevocably in love. It's a symphony that plays the sweet melodies of new beginnings, the somber tones of painful pasts, and the hopeful harmony of a shared future.

This is not just a story of love found through words. It is a story of two worlds merging, two lives unfolding, and two hearts beating in a rhythm as old and sure as the sea itself. It is Lena and Alex's story, a testament to the transformative power of love, the strength of vulnerability, and the profound beauty of choosing to share one's life with another.

Welcome to a tale as deep and boundless as the ocean. Welcome to the love story of Lena and Alex.

Chapter 1

*L*ena's journey to becoming the lighthouse keeper of Havenport was as natural as the changing of the tides. She had grown up in this coastal town, the daughter of a fisherman and a schoolteacher. Her father's tales of the sea had filled her childhood with wonder. While her mother's love of knowledge had instilled in her a deep respect for the quiet power of a well-told story.

The lighthouse had been a central figure in Lena's life since she was a small child. Her family's home was close enough that she fell asleep to its rhythmic flashes each night. The previous keeper, old Mr. Hawthorn, had been like a grandfather to her. Lena learned the details of maintaining the light that protected sailors by spending many afternoons at his side.

When Lena was 16, a storm like no other hit Havenport. Her father's boat was out at sea. The whole town huddled in their homes, praying for the safe return of the fishermen. Lena remembered standing in the lighthouse beside Mr. Hawthorn, who, despite his age, kept the light steady throughout the tempest.

Her father's boat returned safely, guided by the unwavering light. From that moment, Lena knew it intertwined her purpose with the lighthouse. She became Mr. Hawthorn's official apprentice the following summer.

Years passed, and under Mr. Hawthorn's tutelage, Lena became adept at the technical demands of the role. Learning the responsibility that came with it.

Mr. Hawthorn often said, "We don't just keep the light, Lena. We keep the hope."

When Mr. Hawthorn passed away peacefully in his sleep, the town mourned the loss of a steadfast friend. It was with a mix of sadness and honor that Lena stepped into the role she had been preparing for her entire life. The town, knowing her capability and dedication, welcomed her with open arms.

Now, each time she ascends the lighthouse stairs, Lena feels the echoes of Mr. Hawthorn's gentle guidance. She respects the tradition and history of her role but has also made it her own, a beacon of her love for Havenport and her promise to protect those who call it home.

As Lena lights the lamp at dusk, she often whispers a quiet word of gratitude,to the lighthouse. To Mr. Hawthorn, and to the path that led her to become the guardian of this vital flame.

In the soft glow of dawn, Lena ascended the familiar spiral staircase of Havenport Lighthouse. Her hands, weathered but steady, glided over the banister worn smooth by time. She had grown up in this coastal town, the daughter of a fisherman, Samuel, and a schoolteacher, Clara.

"Remember, Lena," her mother used to say during their nightly reading.

"Words are like a lighthouse. They guide us through the dark and stormy nights of life."

Her mother's words always seemed to dance around the room, a warm embrace as a lesson.

One crisp morning, Lena found herself beside her father on his fishing boat.

"Look at that, Lena," Samuel said softly, pointing towards the light-house.

"It's our guiding star. Mr. Hawthorn is more than a keeper of the light. He's a keeper of our safety, our hope."

Lena felt that truth deep in her heart, a call as clear as the bell that tolled in the fog.

Years later, when a tempest threatened to swallow the town whole, Lena stood beside Mr. Hawthorn in the lighthouse. The storm howled like a wounded beast, rain lashing against the windows.

"Steady, Lena," Mr. Hawthorn instructed, his voice firm but kind, as they fought to keep the light burning.

"The town depends on us tonight."

Her father's boat was among those at sea. Lena's hands trembled, but her resolve was ironclad. The light did not falter.

In the following years, Lena apprenticed under Mr. Hawthorn's wise guidance. When he passed, the town mourned, but Lena felt his presence in the lighthouse still, a comforting shadow in her dutiful routine.

Chapter 2

Lena stood at the edge of the rocky coastline, her eyes scanning the horizon as the lighthouse cast its steady glow behind her. Her life was much like this lighthouse: reliable, solitary, and comforting in its routine.

Each morning began with the same rituals. She would rise before the sun, brew a pot of strong coffee, and climb the spiral stairs of the Havenport Lighthouse to clean and polish the glass. From this vantage, she could see the entire sleepy town that had been her world for so many years.

Her afternoons were spent tending to the small garden that flanked the lighthouse, where she grew herbs, vegetables, and vibrant marigolds that mirrored the sunsets. The townspeople, who all knew Lena by name, would often stop by to exchange pleasantries and sometimes trade fresh bread or fish for her ripe tomatoes.

Lena was a figure of constancy in the town. She was the comforting beam that guided fishers safely back to shore and the steady presence that waved to the children as they played near the beach.

In the evenings, after setting the lighthouse and finishing the day's work. Lena would sit in her cozy living room with a book on her lap and her old cat, Whiskers, purring softly beside her. The sounds of the ocean waves crashing against the rocks were a soothing melody that had lulled her to sleep since she was a child.

Today, as Lena looked over the town from her lighthouse, she felt the familiar warmth of contentment. She had watched generations of Havenport residents grow and change from this spot, and yet her own life remained as steady as the tide.

And that was just the way she liked it.

Her peaceful routine was a sanctuary that she had built over the years, and she guarded it with quiet gratitude. She didn't yearn for the noise and rush of a bigger place. Havenport, with its familiar faces and slow, steady rhythm, was home.

This evening, as the sun dipped low and painted the sky with hues of pink and orange, Lena took a deep breath, tasting the salt in the air. She felt a profound connection to this place, a bond forged through years of solitary reflection and service to the town she held so dear.

As she descended the stairs to prepare for another quiet evening, Lena couldn't help but smile.

Chapter 3

Alex sat in a modern, high-rise apartment overlooking a sea of buildings. From the 30th floor, the sprawling city stretched out like an intricate puzzle, its pieces continuously moving. The cacophony from the streets below was a constant companion but inside the meticulously decorated apartment. The acclaimed writer felt a solitude that was suffocating.

His phone buzzed a message from his agent.

"Your next book is due, Alex. The publisher is getting impatient."

The message felt like a cold slap, making his pristine, quiet apartment seem even emptier. Instead of crafting worlds with his words, Alex felt like a prisoner to them. His home, despite being filled with awards and the artifacts of a successful career, felt cold and impersonal.

He wandered to his living room, where his most recent award, an impressive, gleaming trophy, sat on the fireplace mantle. He barely glanced at it. To him, it was just a reminder of the hollow routine his life had become.

He desired authenticity and a deeper connection. But his hectic book signings and surface-level social life couldn't fulfill that wish. As he gazed out of his window at the sprawling urban landscape, he felt the gnawing emptiness expand inside him, as vast and unyielding as the city skyline.

He glanced at a picture on his desk, a photograph of his younger self. Standing on a beach with a smile that reached his eyes, a stark contrast to his reflection in the window now.

In a moment of quiet rebellion and desperation for connection, Alex moved toward his desk and pulled out a sheet of creamy, textured paper. Not for his publisher, but for a stranger.

As he held the pen, he could feel it trembling in his hand, an echo of the turmoil in his heart. This message was his rawest truth, his soul inked on paper. It differed from any story he had written for his adoring readers; this was a story for himself. A confession. A plea.

To whoever finds this,
I am a writer who has run out of words. I filled my life with people, yet I am unbearably alone.
I have crafted countless worlds and breathed life into characters that have touched the hearts of thousands. But when the book closes, when the ink dries, I am left with a hollow ache. My success is an ill-fitting suit; it constrains me and suffocates me.

He paused, taking a deep, steadying breath as he continued,

The city is a temper, constantly swirling around me, but inside my apartment, inside me, it's eerily still. Silent, save for the echoes of my own thoughts, which are often too heavy to bear.
I long for the simple warmth of genuine connection, for a conversation that stretches into the night and makes the soul feel lighter for it. I want to know how the wind feels on your face, what makes you laugh from your belly, and what quiet thoughts visit you before sleep.
If you're reading this, know that I sent this message out like a flare into the night.

He signed it simply with his email address, a digital thread cast into the unknown, a gamble on humanity and hope.

As Alex sealed the message in the bottle, he felt a profound sense of vulnerability, but also a spark of hope that had long been absent. With this act, he was breaking his own isolation. Reaching beyond his self-constructed walls, and allowing himself to hope for a human touch that could heal the raw, open wounds of his soul.

As Alex left his apartment for the first time in days, he felt the door clicking shut behind him like the closing of a chapter. A tangible, resonant end to the isolation he had been nursing. His heart raced in his chest, pulsating like the steady beat of a drum heralding change.

The city that usually felt stifling now seemed to breathe along with him, streets whispering of possibilities as he passed. Every step towards the ocean was a step further from the man he had been, confined within his own walls, both physical and emotional.

The sun was beginning its descent, painting the sky with strokes of gold and crimson. To Alex, it mirrored his own transition; the dark giving way to light, the night yielding to a new day.

As he walked, he clutched the bottle tighter, its solid form a reassuring weight in his hands. It was as if he was holding his own rebirth, his salvation, encapsulated within the glass and sealed with his deepest truths. It felt sacred and terrifying in equal measure.

Reaching the ocean, the gentle lapping of waves greeted him like a soft, welcoming hymn. He stood at the precipice where land met the sea, where certainty met the unknown. He looked out at the vast expanse, feeling both small and infinite at once.

"Is this foolish?" he wondered momentarily, a flicker of doubt crossing his mind.

But then he thought of his letter, of the raw, aching honesty he had poured onto the paper, and he knew he couldn't turn back.

Slowly, he extended his arm, the bottled message poised like a promise in his hand. He felt the salty breeze caress his face, urging him forward as if the world itself was encouraging him. With a deep breath that felt like his first in years, he let go.

As the bottle arced gracefully into the air and towards the water, Alex felt an unraveling within him. A release of the tight coil of loneliness that had been his constant companion. He stood there, on that threshold, and for the first time in a long while, he felt a profound sense of hope.

In that golden, lingering sunset, Alex was not a celebrated author or a city's prisoner. He was a man, vulnerable and open, casting his soul into the world, ready and yearning for the unknown embrace that lay beyond the horizon.

Chapter 4

Walking along the shore after a storm was one of Lena's cherished routines. The salty air, still tinged with the wild energy of the tempest, felt invigorating against her skin. It was a ritual that grounded her, a time when the first light of morning painted the world anew and washed away yesterday's worries.

The stormy sea was a fickle friend; sometimes calm, other times wild and relentless. But it often left behind treasures, shells of iridescent blue, stones. Worn smooth by relentless waves, and driftwood, sculpted by nature into abstract art. These finds were like little secrets the ocean whispered to her, and Lena cherished each one.

On this brisk morning, as the sun cast a golden glow on the wet sand and the retreating tide sang a soft, harmonious tune, something else caught her eye. Amidst the familiar palette of seaweed and stones, a glint of glass beckoned. A bottle, sealed and intact, nestled gently among the rocks, like a pearl in an oyster.

Lena's hands, weathered from years of tending to her lighthouse, reached down with a practiced gentleness. The bottle was cool and slightly wet, kissed by the morning dew. It felt heavy with promise in her hands, and her heart raced in a way it hadn't for years.

Inside, she could see a rolled piece of paper. Not a scrap, but a deliberate message, she could tell. Her eyes widened, and for a moment, she felt like a young girl again, fueled by stories of pirates and mermaids. She looked around, half expecting to see someone watching, to tell her this was part of some elaborate game. But the beach was empty, save for the seagulls that soared and dived in the distance.

The cork came out with a soft *pop*, and as Lena unfurled the paper, her hands trembled slightly. The handwriting was elegant but imbued with palpable emotion. A raw, human earnestness that seemed to leap off the page and resonate with her own solitary soul.

At that moment, with the fresh scent of the ocean filling her lungs and the lighthouse standing tall and steadfast in her peripheral vision. Lena felt a profound connection to this stranger, whose words had journeyed through tempests to find her.

For days, the letter sat on Lena's kitchen table, a silent but powerful presence. It felt like a secret, a window into a stranger's soul that was opened just for her. Every morning, as she sipped her coffee, her eyes would linger on the parchment. It seemed to pulse with a life of its own, like the beating heart of a faraway world.

One overcast afternoon, Lena discussed it with her close friend, Mara, over cups of steaming chamomile tea. Mara's cozy living room was in stark contrast to Lena's minimalist and tranquil lighthouse because of the vibrant paintings and blooming indoor plants adorning it.

"It's like a modern-day message in a bottle," Lena mused, tracing her fingers over the paper. Her voice was soft, almost reverent.

"It's more than that," Mara replied warmly, her eyes filled with empathetic curiosity.

"It's a person reaching out, laying bare their loneliness. What's stopping you from reaching back?"

Lena's gaze drifted to the window, past Mara's garden, and towards the lighthouse that was her world.

"I'm content here," she whispered, a vulnerable quiver in her voice.

"I don't know if I'm ready for a connection that could disrupt that."

"Or enrich it," Mara added gently, reaching out to cover Lena's hands with her own.

"You've given so much light, Lena. Maybe it's time you let some into your own world, too."

Days passed, each one a quiet debate within Lena's heart. She found herself drawn to the email address, penned in smooth handwriting at the bottom of the letter. During her chats with the town's postal worker, Henry, she brought it up.

Henry, with his deep laugh and a salt-and-pepper beard, was a comforting constant in Lena's routine.

"Sounds like fate to me," Henry said with a knowing smile, as he handed Lena a small bundle of mail.

"Your lights guide ships, Lena. Maybe this is someone's light guiding you."

With Henry's words echoing in her mind, Lena felt a resolve solidify within her. She had weathered many storms, both in the sea and in life.

She had learned to embrace solitude, finding peace in the routine of her days and the soothing rhythm of the lighthouse beam. But this? This could be a risk, a storm of change. Yet, wasn't that what life by the sea had taught her? To respect the storms but not to fear them?

After thoughtful evenings tending to her lighthouse, watching the horizon with a newfound sense of longing. And days after letting the letter occupy her thoughts like a tender melody, Lena finally sat down with her computer. Her hands hovered over the keyboard, trembling slightly before she typed a reply to Alex.

Her heart was a tempest, but as she wrote, the storm within her stilled. She felt the warmth of potential friendship, perhaps even love, seeping into her words, chasing away the chill of her routine solitude.

Chapter 5

Sitting at her computer, Lena felt a nervous flutter in her stomach, a sensation akin to the wild, unpredictable winds before a storm. Her fingers, usually steady from years of tending to her lighthouse, hovered hesitantly over the keyboard. This was uncharted territory, a step into someone else's world, a leap of faith she had never expected to take.

Her quaint kitchen was softly lit, her home a bastion of warmth against the cool evening air outside. It filled the room with the comforting scent of tea, a daily ritual, but today it felt like a companion at this significant moment.

With a deep breath, she typed,

Subject: A Reply from the Lighthouse
"Dear Alex,
Your words found their way to me, across vast seas and under a lighthouse's watchful eye. I hope this email finds you in kinder spirits than when you penned your letter.
Warmly,
Lena"

She reviewed the email, simple, yet infused with a warmth she hoped would resonate through the screen. Her heart, a rhythm she rarely noticed, drummed loudly in her ears as if echoing the gravity of the moment.

With each second, Lena could feel the pull of a strange but compelling connection, a curiosity she hadn't felt in years. Alex's vulnerability had touched something within her. Awakened, a part of her soul she had kept reserved only for her lighthouse and the endless horizon. It was terrifying and exhilarating all at once.

As her gaze drifted towards the window, she could see her beloved lighthouse standing tall and steadfast in the distance. It was her grounding point, her constant, a symbol of her chosen solitude, but now it also felt like a beacon calling her to a new adventure.

With a final, steadying breath, as deep and bracing as the ocean winds, Lena pressed send. She imagined the digital message soaring away. Much like the bottle had on its oceanic journey, an ethereal vessel, now charting a course for unknown waters.

In that quiet instant, after the click of the mouse and before the uncertainty of a reply, Lena felt a serene clarity. No matter where this correspondence might lead, she sensed, deep in her bones, that her world had just expanded beyond the rocky shores of her coastal town.

Chapter 6

The following morning, as the first light of dawn painted the sky in hues of pink and gold, Lena sat with her steaming mug of tea at the kitchen table. It was a ritual, this quiet time before her duties at the lighthouse began, a sacred space of solitude that Lena had always cherished.

As she opened her laptop, her heart did an unexpected leap.

New Message. Alex's name, now a digital signature, was startling in its presence, a beacon that seemed to brighten her quiet morning in ways she hadn't expected.

Subject: Re: A Reply from the Lighthouse
"Dear Lena,
I had hoped but hardly dared to believe, that my bottle would find a kindred spirit. Your email was a light in my day. Tell me, what is it like living under the watch of a lighthouse?
Sincerely,
Alex"

Reading Alex's words, Lena felt an unexpected warmth spread through her chest, like a cozy blanket on a chilly morning. She could sense his relief and gratitude in the phrasing, the raw sincerity that radiated from his words. It was a sentiment Lena had rarely encoun-tered; she found it disarmingly honest and incredibly endearing.

She looked towards her lighthouse, visible from her window, standing like an old friend against the coastal landscape. How could she encapsulate what that life was like in words?

The comforting routine, the quiet but fulfilling solitude, the way the sea spoke to her soul. It was a symphony she lived daily but had never tried to put into words, especially not for someone else.

As she pondered, Lena realized that Alex's simple question was an invitation. An opening for her to share a part of her life that was as natural to her as breathing, yet deeply intimate. It was an opportunity for her to glimpse into his world, equally foreign yet suddenly signifi-cant.

Taking another sip of her tea, Lena could feel the texture of the moment; it was fragile and beautiful, laden with potential. Here, in this quiet dawn with the day awakening around her, Lena wasn't just the lighthouse keeper.

She was Lena, the woman on the verge of a profound connection, about to share her world with someone who genuinely wanted to know.

With renewed resolve and her heart beating a lively, hopeful rhythm, Lena placed her fingers back on the keys. She was ready to illuminate her world for Alex, just as his message had brought a new light into hers.

Chapter 7

A lex sat in his high-rise apartment. the towering buildings outside his window making him feel both connected to a sprawling metropolis and profoundly isolated at the same time. His home, a modern marvel with sleek lines and glass surfaces, mirrored his recent novels: polished but lacking the heart that once fueled his writing.

Alex's days, once filled with passionate writing sessions, had become predictable. Wake up, try to write, stare at the blinking cursor, get lost in the city noise, and attempt to silence his loneliness with the bustling social scene of book launches and writer panels. The intimate, authentic interactions he used to treasure had turned into rehearsed conversations with industry acquaintances.

When he sent that message in a bottle, it was an act of quiet rebellion. A desperate attempt to reach out, to feel again, to connect with someone beyond the confines of his screen and the cold cityscape.

As he sat at his desk, Alex was trying not to hope. But every time his email notification pinged, his heart raced uncontrollably.

And then, there it was, a new message with a subject line that made his heart swell.

"A Reply from the Lighthouse." *

"Dear Lena,

I had hoped but hardly dared to believe, that my bottle would find a
kindred spirit. Your email was a light in my day. Tell me, what is it like
living under the watch of a lighthouse?
Sincerely,
Alex"

As he typed his reply, Alex felt something crack open within him. A softening, a relief that made his eyes well with tears he hadn't expected. For the first time in what felt like forever, he was engaging in a conversation that wasn't dictated by deadlines or publishers.

He was speaking to a soul who lived in a world so different from his, yet will reach across that divide.

Alex pictured Lena in her coastal abode. Living a life paced by the rhythm of the sea, he yearned. Not for a change of scenery, but for that same authentic, unhurried connection with another human being.

He envisioned her lighthouse as a steadfast guardian. In his loneliest moments, he imagined that light reaching all the way to him, cutting through the dense fog of his urban isolation.

Each word he wrote to Lena was tinged with a vulnerability and hope he had long forgotten, but now eagerly embraced. In Lena, in this surprising and serendipitous correspondence, Alex saw a possibility, a chance to rediscover not just the joy of connection, but perhaps the path back to his own authentic voice and heart.

Chapter 8

In her cozy living room, with a view of the waves crashing gently against the rocks, Lena carefully crafted her emails to Alex. They were her daily ritual now, composed with the same care and attention she gave to maintaining her beloved lighthouse.

"The lighthouse feels like a part of my soul. Its steadfast presence, its rhythm, and routine, ground me.
Every time I light its lamp, I feel like I'm sending a beacon of hope into the night.
It's not just about guiding ships, it's a connection to something bigger than myself.
What fuels your writing, Alex?"

She could feel her heart racing as she pressed send, the excitement of reaching out to Alex never dimming.

Back in the city, Alex sat in his once lonely apartment, now warmed by Lena's virtual presence. Her emails were the first thing he looked for in the morning and the last thing he read at night. They were his solace in a world that often felt too harsh and demanding.

In response to Lena's question, he opened up more than he ever had before, not as a celebrated author, but as Alex, the man behind the words.

For a long time, my writing was a shield. It was a world I could control when everything else seemed chaotic.
But as the years have passed, it's become more of a bridge than a barrier.
It's a way for me to explore humanity, emotions, and truth.
Our conversations, Lena, have been fueling it lately. You make me want to capture the raw, honest beauty of life, the kind I feel when I read your words.

As Lena read Alex's email, she felt a surge of warmth that she hadn't known in years. His honesty, his vulnerability, mirrored her own. She felt seen In a way she hadn't expected, and it was simultaneously exhilarating and terrifying.

Sitting with her steaming cup of tea, she read and re-read Alex's words. Each sentence felt like a brushstroke of a painting they were creating together. A vibrant, intricate portrait of two lives intertwining despite the miles between them.

"Alex," she typed, her fingers steady but her heart fluttering.

Your words are like a lighthouse to me, too.
They guide me through my own storms and make the world feel a little less vast and intimidating.
I never expected this, but I'm incredibly grateful for it.

Chapter 9

The café was a tapestry of aromas, freshly brewed coffee, buttery pastries, and Mara's floral perfume. It was a comfort to Lena, almost as grounding as her lighthouse. She looked up from Alex's email and met Mara's steady gaze, her own eyes reflecting a mix of wonder and apprehension.

"You light up when you talk about him, Lena," Mara observed, her tone rich with warmth.

She had known Lena through all life's chapters, the joyful, the mundane, and the painful, and this was a look on her friend she hadn't seen in years.

Lena's eyes darted back to the screen, where Alex's words danced before her, personal and poetic.

"It's... it's more," she whispered, the words heavy with vulnerability.

"He writes with a rawness that echoes in me. His words are like a melody I didn't know I was missing. But it terrifies me, Mara. What if this all crumbles and I'm left with that absence again?"

Mara moved gracefully, her familiarity with the café clear in every step. She sat beside Lena, her presence steadfast and calming.

"Life is full of 'what ifs', dear friend," she replied gently, her hand enveloping Lena's in a reassuring grasp.

"But 'what ifs' aren't what we live for. Look at you, you've built a life around guiding others through darkness and storm. Maybe this is your chance to let someone else be your guide for a change."

Lena's tears were soft and warm, a cathartic release she hadn't allowed herself in years. The café sounds blurred into the background, and in that moment, the room seemed to hold only her and Mara, as if the world had given them this sacred space.

"You've always been brave," Mara whispered, brushing a tear from Lena's cheek with the back of her hand.

"In your own quiet way, you've been braver than anyone I know. Alex isn't a storm, Lena, he's a new chapter, and you're the author as much as he is. Write it fearlessly."

In that tender moment, Lena felt the weight of Mara's love and wisdom anchoring her. She realized she wasn't facing the unknown alone; she had her lifelong friend by her side, and maybe, just maybe, she had Alex too.

Chapter 10

In the soft glow of his apartment's carefully chosen light, Alex sat at his desk. A space that had once felt like a fortress, where he fortified himself from the world outside. But now, in this quiet moment, it felt different. It felt softer, warmer, more alive, much like Alex himself felt these days. Each email from Lena was like a sunbeam cutting through the fog that had clouded his life.

He re-read Lena's last message, her inquiries about his work feeling genuinely curious and caring, not probing or critical like the questions he was used to from interviews and fans. Lena saw him as Alex, not just the name on a book cover.

"For a long time," he wrote, his fingers moving over the keys with a fluency that felt as natural as breathing.

My writing was a shield.
It was my suit of armor in a world that seemed intent on breaking me down.
It was a space where I was in control when everything else felt like it was spiraling.

He paused, his eyes drifting to the window. The city's skyline once a reminder of his isolation among millions. Now seemed to hold a different promise, a world vast enough for unexpected, beautiful connections like the one he was nurturing with Lena.

"*But as the years have passed,*" he continued, each word echoing the profound truth within his heart.

Writing has become more of a bridge than a barrier.
It's how I seek to understand people, emotions, the world, and myself. I
It's less about escaping now and more about connecting, about probing
the deep and sometimes dark corners of the human experience.

He hesitated before adding the next sentence, the vulnerability in it making his heart race. But Lena's sincerity had invited his own, time and time again.

"*Lately,*" Alex confessed.

"Our conversations have fueled it, Lena.
You bring richness, and depth to my days that I didn't realize was missing.
You make me want to write not just as a means of expression but to capture the raw, honest beauty of life, the kind I feel when I read your words.
Your presence, even in this digital form, has become a lighthouse in my world."

As Alex pressed send, his heartbeat resonated in his chest like a drum, echoing the gravity of the moment. He realized that this wasn't just another email; it was an invitation into his inner world, a space he had fiercely guarded for years. With every word he had typed, he was peeling back layers of himself that few had ever seen.

He looked at the sent message on his screen, the words "Message Sent" feeling more like a proclamation than a simple notification.

It was a declaration that he had stepped over a threshold that there was no crossing back from. He was allowing himself to be seen in all his aspirations and vulnerabilities. Not just as a celebrated writer, but as Alex, a man with dreams, fears, and a yearning for connection.

He sat back in his chair and took a deep breath, feeling it as though for the first time. The air was fresh, lighter, yet charged with possibility. It was as if, in opening himself up to Lena, he was also opening a new chapter for himself. One filled not with the expected plot points of a solitary author's life. With the unpredictable and thrilling narrative of genuine human connection.

As he looked around his apartment, the space seemed to reflect his internal transformation. The shelves of books, once his steadfast companions in solitude, now felt like witnesses to this profound moment of change. His awards, which once defined his worth in his own eyes, seemed to quietly recede into the background.

Making space for something far more valuable, authenticity and connection.

For the first time in a long time, Alex felt grounded, not confined by the walls of his apartment. Anchored by a deep sense of self and purpose that Lena's correspondence had helped to ignite within him. Simultaneously, he felt free, like a bird taking its first daring flight from the nest. Carried by winds of trust and openness that he had only understood.

At that moment, he recognized the profound strength Lena's own vulnerability had imparted to him. Her openness was not a sign of weakness, as he might have once thought, but a courageous act of strength, one that inspired him to be brave in kind.

He leaned back further in his chair, allowing himself to bask in this unfamiliar sensation. A smile, pure and unguarded, graced his lips. Alex realized that, in reaching out to Lena, he wasn't just seeking companionship; he was actively rewriting his own story, allowing for a richer narrative filled with connection, vulnerability, and undiscovered depths of emotion.

Chapter 11

In a brightly lit office in the city's heart, Sam, Alex's longtime editor, and friend, was growing concerned. He had been through countless book cycles with Alex and had seen the difficulties, but this time was different. The usually punctual and prolific writer was missing deadlines, and Sam could sense that something was off.

"Alex," Sam began, choosing his words carefully as they sat across from each other in Sam's office.

"The publisher is anxious. We need to get this book rolling. Is everything okay? You've seemed... distant lately."

Alex looked up, his eyes betraying a weariness that hadn't been there a few months ago. Work, once his dominant passion and solace, was now a source of stress that clashed with the newfound joy Lena brought into his life.

"I know, Sam," Alex sighed deeply, running his fingers through his hair.

"It's just... I've met someone, in a way. We've been writing to each other, and it's... it's different. She's different. She makes me want to live differently."

Sam's stern expression softened into one of empathy. He had known Alex for years and understood how significant this admission was.

"That's incredible, Alex," Sam replied warmly.

"But you know this world. We have commitments, contracts, and deadlines. We can't just put everything on hold."

"I understand that," Alex responded, a tightness forming in his chest.

"But these emails with Lena, they're... they're the most genuine thing in my life right now. I feel torn, Sam. How do I balance this?"

Sam leaned forward, placing his hands on the table, grounding the moment.

"Alex, life is about finding that balance," he advised earnestly.

"Don't lose yourself in the pressures of this industry. If Lena is important, which it sounds like she is. You'll need to carve out space for her, for this new connection. But you also have a gift, Alex. A gift that the world wants and needs. It's possible to have both, but it's up to you to find that equilibrium."

Alex nodded slowly, absorbing Sam's words. He felt the weight of the decision he faced. Could he cultivate this burgeoning, life-changing relationship with Lena while also meeting the demands of his career, a career that, until Lena, had been his entire world? It was a question without simple answers, and he felt the strain of being caught between two worlds.

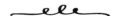

In the quiet hours of that evening, Alex sat alone in his apartment. The golden glow of streetlights outside his window painted the room with a warmth that contrasted with the cold reality he was grappling with. The empty, white document on his computer screen stared back at him, an unwritten chapter of his next book, and a symbol of the path he had always known.

He closed his eyes and took a deep breath, Lena's latest email vivid in his mind. Her words, always imbued with the gentle cadence of her personality, were like a soothing melody that reached him in this time of turmoil. She had shared the simple joys of her day, the soft colors of dawn over the sea, and her quiet reflections as she maintained the lighthouse. Her world was a stark contrast to his, but in her words, he found a serenity he had long forgotten.

Alex's phone buzzed on the table, pulling him from his thoughts. It was a reminder from Sam, a gentle nudge about the looming deadline. A wave of anxiety washed over him, but it also brought clarity.

He knew he couldn't abandon his writing. It was a part of him, as essential as breathing. But he also couldn't ignore the profound connection he had found with Lena. It was as if, in meeting her, even just through words, he was meeting a part of himself he hadn't known was missing.

At that moment, he decided. He would write, not just for deadlines or publishers, but for himself and for Lena. He would pour the honesty and love he felt in his correspondence with her into his work. His writing would be a testament to this delicate, powerful balance he was striving to achieve between his love for Lena and his passion for storytelling.

With newfound determination, Alex's fingers found their way to the keyboard. As he typed, the words flowed like a river, inspired, genuine, and imbued with the depth of his experiences and emotions.

For the first time in what felt like an eternity, Alex felt harmonious, as if the disparate parts of his life were finally beautifully converging.

Chapter 12

One sunny afternoon, Lena found herself in Mara's café again, but her radiant friend could see the storm in Lena's eyes. They sat in their usual corner, surrounded by the comforting scent of fresh coffee and the soft murmur of townspeople enjoying their day.

"You've been distant lately," Mara observed gently, reaching across the table to place her hand over Lena's.

"You're not physically here, but your mind seems miles away."

Lena sighed deeply, her gaze fixed on the steaming cup before her.

"I'm scared, Mara," she admitted, her voice trembling slightly.

"I feel like I'm standing on the edge of a precipice with Alex. I've never cared for someone in this way, and it's terrifying. What if everything changes?"

As they spoke, Henry, the town's postman, approached their table with his usual warm smile.

"Lena," he greeted warmly.

"I couldn't help but overhear. Change can be a blessing, you know. It's a chance to grow."

At that moment, a skeptical voice chimed in from a nearby table. It was Eleanor, a longtime resident known for her traditional views.

"Or it's a chance to lose oneself," she countered sharply, eyeing Lena with concern.

"We've known you since you were a child, Lena. This man is a stranger. What do you really know about him?"

Lena felt a sting at Eleanor's words, but also a twinge of truth. She had built a life here, a routine that brought her peace and purpose. Alex's presence, as comforting as it was, had also brought unrest, a shifting in the tides of her life that was both exhilarating and frightening.

Seeing Lena's struggle, Mara squeezed her friend's hand reassuringly.

"Lena," Mara whispered, her voice steady and soothing.

"We don't love because it's safe. We love it because it feels right because it's a leap we're willing to take. Trust your heart. It's led you well so far."

Lena felt the collective care of her town, those who wanted to protect her, and those encouraging her leap of faith. With a deep breath, she realized that whatever decision she made; it had to be hers alone.

In that breath, she felt a clarity emerge from her storm of doubts. It was like the moment after a tempest when the sea calms and the path is clear once more. She looked up at Mara, her eyes brighter now, brimming not with fear, but with resolve.

"I've spent my life guiding others safely through storms," Lena said, her voice steady and imbued with a newfound strength.

"It's time for me to navigate my course."

Mara's eyes welled with tears, her smile reflecting both pride and deep affection for her friend.

"Then set your sails, Lena," she replied warmly.

"Wherever this journey takes you, know that we are your harbor, always here when you need to anchor."

In her heart, Lena knew the lighthouse had taught her more than guiding ships, it had taught her about guiding her own way in life, too.

And with that, she was ready to embrace the uncertain, promising horizon that lay before her with Alex.

Chapter 13

In his latest email, Alex carefully chose his words, crafting a question that felt as monumental as any pivotal scene in his novels. He could sense Lena's hesitation in her last few messages. The fear of change was clear, but he also felt the undeniable bond that had grown between them.

"Dear Lena," he typed, the cursor blinking like a heartbeat on the screen.
"Our words have crossed oceans, bringing warmth and understanding I never expected.
I feel as though I've come to know not only the lighthouse keeper in her tower, but the woman with dreams, fears, and a heart as vast as the sea.
I don't want our story to be confined to screens and keys."

He paused, taking a deep breath, as if he could somehow convey the depth of his sincerity through the keys.
"What would you say," he continued,

"to us meeting in person?
I understand the weight of this proposal, and I want you to know there is no pressure.

Only hope for a new chapter, for both of us."

As Alex pressed send, his heart seemed to synchronize with the rhythm of the blinking cursor, each beat echoing the gravity of his words. This wasn't just a message; it was an invitation, a path potentially leading to a future neither of them could have scripted.

In this quiet room, surrounded by the artifacts of his successful but once lonely existence, the profound sense of hope he now felt was palpable, almost transformative.

His fingers, which had crafted worlds and characters, trembled slightly, a raw, human response that his protagonist's stoic demeanor rarely betrayed. For a man accustomed to plotting every twist and turn in his stories, this step into the unknown was both terrifying and exhilarating.

He could imagine Lena reading his words under the soft glow of her lighthouse, the salt air mingling with her surprise, her joy, or her apprehension. He could almost see her eyes, wide and luminous, reflecting the same mix of vulnerability and hope that he himself was grappling with.

At that moment, as he sat alone but for the soft hum of his computer, Alex realized he was, in a way, standing at his own shoreline, casting this deeply personal message into the currents of Lena's world.

It was a surrender to fate, to possibility, to love, and to the painful, beautiful act of reaching out to another human being, without map or compass, guided only by the stars of their shared connection.

And so, with his heart laid bare and his future uncertain, Alex waited, for a reply, for a chance, for Lena's guiding light to beckon him closer or signal a course change. In this suspenseful pause, he understood that he was not alone; across the sea, Lena was navigating this emotional tempest with him.

Chapter 14

When Lena saw the notification for a new email from Alex, her heart skipped a beat, as it always did. But today was different. Before even opening it, she could sense the weight this message carried. Her hands were slightly shaky as she moved her cursor to click it open.

The subject line read, *"A Proposal of Sorts,"* and as she read Alex's words, inviting her to meet in person. A powerful tide of emotions, including excitement, fear, joy, and apprehension, blended into a rush that momentarily stilled the world around Lena.

Her eyes widened, and she read and re-read the email, each word echoing in her mind like a melody. His vulnerability was mirrored in her own racing heart and the warmth spreading through her chest. This was the leap of faith, the crossing of their two worlds that she had both longed for and feared.

In her cozy kitchen, with the comforting sound of waves outside and the lighthouse casting its steadfast beam into the dark, Lena felt the magnitude of Alex's gesture. Here, in her sanctuary, the decision she faced was as vast and deep as the ocean itself.

She looked out of her window towards the lighthouse, her constant companion and symbol of her life's purpose. Could she invite someone into this world she cherished? Was she ready to step into the unfamiliar territory that lay beyond her shores?

Lena clasped her hands together, grounding herself. She knew that in her reply; she held the power to either draw their two worlds closer or to maintain the life she had known and loved. It was a choice that carried both the promise of new love and the risk of profound change.

Taking a deep breath, Lena allowed herself to consume the significance of this moment. She closed her eyes and pictured Alex, whom she had come to know so intimately through their words, their shared dreams, and their vulnerabilities. She envisioned his face, his smile, the kindness in his eyes that she felt in every line he wrote.

Opening her eyes, Lena saw her own reflection in the window, strong, yet with a softness that had deepened since knowing Alex. She saw, too, in the lighthouse's beam, the steady pulse that was her life's work and passion.

She thought of her friend Mara, her encouraging words about embracing unexpected gifts, and Henry, who'd likened Alex's message to a guiding light.

With renewed clarity, Lena began to type her response. Each word was deliberate, carrying the weight of her decision, but also the warmth of her feelings for Alex:

"Dear Alex,

Your proposal took my breath away, in the most wonderful way. I've grown so fond of you, and I feel a connection I didn't think was possible through mere words on a screen. Meeting you felt like the most natural next step, a chapter I am ready and eager to explore.

Let's bridge our worlds, Alex. Let's meet.

Warmest wishes, Lena"

As she pressed send, Lena felt a profound sense of peace. It was a leap, but she was leaping with her whole heart, ready for whatever story lay ahead with Alex.

As she pressed send, Lena felt as though she were stepping into a new world, one rich with possibility and vivid with color. The familiar room around her seemed to hum with the weight of this moment, the gentle whir of her computer, the distant call of seabirds outside, and the rhythmic pulse of the lighthouse beacon beyond her window.

Her whole life, she had been a steadfast beacon for others, guiding, and watching, but always rooted in place. Now, in her decision to reach toward Alex, she was allowing herself to be drawn into a new and uncertain journey. It was both exhilarating and terrifying.

Her heart, usually as steady as her lighthouse, fluttered wildly in her chest. It wasn't just anticipation she was feeling; it was transformation. In choosing Alex, she wasn't turning away from her life, but expanding it, inviting in warmth, connection, and a shared path that she never allowed herself to imagine before.

Chapter 15

A s Alex stepped off the train into the coastal town, his heart raced like the rolling waves he could hear in the distance. The quaint cobblestone streets and the scent of salt in the air felt both foreign and intimately familiar, painted so vividly through Lena's words that he felt he'd walked these streets before in his dreams.

He caught sight of Lena before she saw him. She was exactly as he had pictured, her posture mirroring the strength and grace she carried in her emails. Her eyes, the color of the sea at dusk, scanned the crowd nervously.

In that moment, Alex felt a profound vulnerability; he was no longer just words on a screen but a man, standing before her, teeming with hope and fear.

Their meeting was beautifully, painfully awkward. Lena, her warmth radiating even from a distance, reached out for a hug, but her arms hesitated mid-air, second-guessing the intimacy of that gesture.

Alex, wanting to bridge the gap but equally uncertain, extended his hand for a handshake, then chuckled at the stiffness of it under the weight of their shared history.

Hearing his laugh, a sound she knew in her imagination, now rich and real before her, Lena's shoulders relaxed, and she closed the distance, wrapping him in a heartfelt embrace.

Alex touched to his core, and responded in kind, his arms encircling her with a warmth that felt like home.

In that embrace, Alex's nerves quieted.

"It's beyond words, finally meeting you," he whispered, his voice trembling with the enormity of the moment.

He could feel her nod against his shoulder, her breath steady but deep, as if she was anchoring herself in this new reality.

Lena smiled warmly as they stepped back, tears pooling in her eyes, making them shine brighter than he'd imagined.

"And you," she whispered, her voice rich with emotion.

"Feel like a story I've known my whole life, but am only now beginning to read."

They lingered at that moment, neither rushing to fill the space. It was a profound, shared pause, honoring the incredible journey that led to this meeting, two souls, finally entwined after crossing vast emotional and physical distances, ready to explore the unwritten chapters that lay ahead together.

Chapter 16

The drive to Alex's hotel made them feel a sense of tangible reality that they had never experienced before. Inside the car, a comforting warmth emanated from the heater, contrasting the cool, salt-tinged air outside.

As Lena maneuvered down the familiar winding roads of her coastal town, the headlights illuminated the path ahead, much like the lighthouse she tended to, casting its guiding light.

Alex sat in the passenger seat, absorbing the quaint charm of Lena's world, the cozy houses nestled among the dunes. The quiet streets echoed with the song of the sea. It was a stark, yet soothing contrast to the bustling city he hailed from.

He turned to watch Lena as she drove, admiring the way her eyes focused on the road, yet occasionally met his with a soft and appreciative glance.

Lena, aware of Alex's thoughtful gaze, felt a serene comfort in his presence. The nervous energy that had accompanied their first meeting was gradually giving way to a sense of companionship that felt as natural as the rhythmic sound of the waves outside.

"This town," she began softly.

"It's more than a home. It's my heart. I hope that, through me, it can become a part of your world too."

Alex's reply was warm, his voice a tender echo in the space between them.

"Seeing it through your eyes," he said.

"It already feels like a place I could belong. It's beautiful, Lena, just like the soul you've shared with me through our words."

As they approached the charming, old-world hotel Alex had booked. A beautiful stone building with ivy crawling up its sides, they shared a peaceful, charged moment, recognizing the significance of this journey they were embarking on together.

Lena parked the car and turned off the engine, but neither of them was in a rush to break the connection. Instead, they lingered, allowing the weight and promise of the moment to settle warmly around them, cherishing the physical closeness that their digital correspondence had finally, beautifully, led to.

As Lena turned to face Alex, her eyes, the color of the deep sea after a storm, met his, warm and brown like aged leather. In her gaze, Alex saw the resilience and grace of a woman who had learned to dance with the tempests, both literal and metaphorical.

Her skin, kissed by the salt air and sun, carried a natural glow, and her dark hair, pulled back to reveal a thoughtful face, adjusted with the breeze that slipped through the car window. In that moment, he saw not just the lighthouse keeper, but the woman who had breathed life into her words, painting vivid images that kept him anchored during his own internal storms.

For Lena, looking into Alex's eyes was like peering into a comforting novel. His eyes were expressive, telling stories she was eager to read and understand. His face, framed by a thoughtful trim of beard, carried an inviting warmth, softened further by the gentle smile that seemed to live there naturally when he looked at her.

His hands, which had crafted the words that reached into her world, were strong yet gentle, resting patiently in his lap. In him, Lena saw a profound depth and sensitivity, the soul of a writer and a dreamer whose vulnerability and strength had mingled with her own through every exchanged line and paragraph.

In that charged, intimate pause, they felt as though they were both authors and readers in a story that was unfolding in real-time, each taking in the details, the nuances, the very essence of the other, recognizing the deep connection that had grown between them and was now, finally, crossing the boundary from words on a screen to a tangible, promising reality.

Chapter 17

In that quiet, electric moment between them, Lena and Alex leaned closer, as if drawn together by an invisible force neither could resist. Their faces, reflecting nervous excitement and genuine affection, slowly closed the remaining space between them.

It was a movement as natural as the ebb and flow of the tide, years of loneliness and longing culminating in this single, defining instant.

As their lips finally met, there was a profound tenderness in their connection. It was a kiss imbued with all the words they had shared and all the emotions they had poured into their correspondence, a kiss that was at once both a hello and a promise, delicate but with an undercurrent of deep, unspoken intensity.

In that kiss, they tasted each other's worlds, the salty breeze of Lena's coastal home, and the warm, comforting notes of Alex's worn books. They confirmed their emotional journey with a kiss, which physically manifested their bond.

Heartfelt exchanges across miles and time zones had nurtured this bond.

With that simple yet profound act, Lena and Alex embraced the risk and beauty of their new chapter together, knowing they were both ready to navigate this uncharted path with each other's hearts as their guiding light.

As they pulled up to the hotel, the warmth of their recent kiss still lingering between them, Alex turned to Lena, his eyes tender but tinged with a hint of vulnerability. He smiled gently, his words measured as he navigated this delicate, unfamiliar terrain.

"Do you... would you like to come up to my room?" he asked, his voice softer than before.

"Just to talk," he quickly added, a hint of nervous laughter in his tone as he sought to ease any pressure.

"And maybe continue what we've started, in person and without the screen between us."

Lena looked into his eyes, finding there the same sincerity that had won her heart through emails.

She saw in his awkwardness not a presumption, but a genuine desire to deepen their connection and continue their conversation, a chance to sit side by side after months of anticipation.

In that moment, as Lena considered his invitation, it was clear they both understood the significance of this step; not just a casual extension of their evening, but a conscious move towards further intimacy and trust in their unfolding love story.

Chapter 18

In the hotel room, the atmosphere was a tender mix of familiar and new. They had shared so much already, unveiling their souls through words, and now, for the first time, they were physically sharing the same space. The room was softly lit, casting a warm glow that seemed to mirror their internal connection.

Alex, ever the thoughtful host despite being the visitor, gestured to a chair by a small table.

"Please, make yourself comfortable," he said, his voice steady but carrying an undercurrent of excitement.

Lena smiled appreciatively and moved gracefully across the room, her presence filling the space in a way that made it feel instantly more like home for both of them. As she sat, she still held onto the tangible, electric charge between them, felt feeling profoundly at ease, as if she had known this room, this moment, and this man for far longer than she actually had.

They exchanged glances that spoke volumes, their eyes reflecting both the depth of their emotional journey and the novelty of this physical closeness.

In this intimate setting, every slight gesture.

Alex's hands as they brushed a lock of hair behind his ear, Lena's soft laugh that seemed to light up the room, felt imbued with significance, and the air between them was charged with anticipation.

In this room, away from the world, they talked just as openly as they had in their emails. Their conversation flowed naturally, with the effortless grace that comes when two people are genuinely in tune.

They shared stories, laughed, and occasionally reached out to touch, an affirming hand on the other's arm, a tender brush of fingers that felt as natural and significant as the words they were exchanging.

As they sat there, deep into the night, the room became a sanctuary for their burgeoning connection, a space where they could, at last, fully intertwine their lives that had for so long been separated by miles and screens.

In the soft light of the room, Lena could see the sincerity and warmth in Alex's eyes, which had often come through in his words but were infinitely more potent now, in person. They were the eyes of someone who had known solitude and was now, cautiously but hopefully, opening his world to someone else.

She noticed the subtle signs of his nervousness that betrayed his otherwise composed demeanor, the way he occasionally looked down and smiled shyly, the earnest way he held her gaze when he spoke like he was absorbing every word she said as though it were a precious gem.

Alex, in turn, was captivated by Lena. In her, he saw a soul as deep and vast as the sea she lived by. He noticed the way her eyes sparkled when she talked about her beloved lighthouse, the passionate cadence of her voice when she shared her dreams and the way she laughed, full-hearted and genuine.

The small, unconscious gestures she made as she spoke struck him, like tucking a strand of her hair behind her ear or the soft way she would touch her lips when lost in thought. He realized that each of these gestures was a brushstroke in the portrait of a woman he had grown to care for deeply through their correspondence, and now even more profoundly in person.

As the night wore on, the initial nerves that accompanied their meeting seemed to dissolve, leaving in their place a deep sense of comfort and intimacy. They found themselves leaning closer, the space between them charged with a palpable connection that neither had experienced before in such a profound way.

In a quiet lull in the conversation, Alex gently reached out and brushed his fingers against Lena's cheek, a question in his eyes that was met with warmth in hers. It was in that tender moment, surrounded by the soft glow of the room, that they shared their second kiss, a kiss that was equal parts sweet, passionate, and profound.

It was a kiss that seemed to hold within it all the words they had shared and all the future words they would exchange, a promise and an anchor in their new, shared journey.

After the kiss, they pulled back slightly, just enough to see each other's faces, but remained close, close enough that they could feel each other's breath. They shared a look of deep affection and understanding, a silent acknowledgment that what they were building was both extraordinary and real.

"No matter what comes next," Alex whispered, his voice full of emotion.

"This moment, here with you, feels like the most honest thing I've ever known."

Lena's eyes welled with tears at his heartfelt words, and she whispered back.

"For me, too, Alex. For me, too."

In that instant, they both knew that their lives had irrevocably changed, and they were ready to embrace that change together.

Chapter 19

As dawn painted the room with a soft, golden light, Lena and Alex lay entwined in each other's arms, neither having slept much but both feeling more rested than they had in ages. The room, which just hours before had been a realm of unknowns, now felt like a sacred space, a cocoon that had nurtured their connection from the digital to the tangible.

Lena, nestled against Alex's chest, listened to the steady rhythm of his heartbeat. It was a comforting sound, a rhythmic affirmation of the reality of his presence. She felt his hand gently stroking her hair, each movement a silent vow, grounding them in this new day.

For Alex, holding Lena felt like holding a missing piece of himself he didn't know he had been searching for. Her warmth was a balm to the lingering cold he had grown accustomed to in his solitary life. He could feel her breathing, steady and serene, and it brought an unprecedented sense of calm to his own often restless mind.

As they lay there in the morning's quietude, the weight of the world outside that room felt both distant and irrelevant. All that mattered was that they were here, together, in this moment that neither of them had dared to imagine, but now couldn't fathom living without.

Eventually, Lena lifted her head and met Alex's eyes, her own reflecting a mix of joy, vulnerability, and love.

"Good morning," she whispered, her voice carrying a depth of emotion that made the greeting feel like so much more.

Alex responded with a tender smile, his eyes mirroring her own complex blend of feelings.

"Good morning," he replied softly, the warmth in his tone wrapping around her like a gentle embrace.

"It's a new day," he added, "our new day."

Chapter 20

In the weeks following Alex's arrival, Lena noticed the subtle yet significant changes in the rhythms of her town. It started with the small things; Alex holding the door for the bustling mothers at the local bakery, his laughter blending into the Saturday morning chatter at the farmers' market, and the sight of him sitting beside Lena on the porch of her lighthouse home, his pen dancing over the paper as the sun dipped below the horizon.

Mara, ever the attentive friend, was the first to articulate the shift she saw in Lena. One evening, as they closed up the café together, she turned to Lena with a knowing smile.

"I see the way he looks at you," she said, her voice rich with warmth.

"And I see the way you look at him, Lena. It's like he's not just visiting here, but becoming a part of this place. Just like he's becoming a part of you."

Lena's eyes welled with tears of gratitude.

"He's teaching me how to love without fear," she replied softly.

"And this town, our friends, they're teaching him about belonging, about community. We're learning from each other, growing together."

Meanwhile, Alex had been embraced in ways he hadn't expected. The town's fisherman, a gruff yet kind man named Thomas, had taken a liking to Alex, inviting him on early morning fishing excursions.

Alex, initially a stranger to the tides and knots, soon shared stories with Thomas as they sailed beneath the predawn sky, the lighthouse beam a constant, reassuring presence.

One significant Sunday, the townspeople invited Alex to speak at the local community hall, a tradition reserved for those considered part of the town's family. Alex stood at the front of the hall, Lena's supportive hand in his, and shared his journey, not as a celebrated author, but as a man who had found his way home to love and through this town.

As Lena looked out at the faces of her neighbors, her friends, and her world, she saw their expressions mirroring her own joy and acceptance. She saw Mrs. Ellington nodding thoughtfully, Mara's eyes shimmering with tears of happiness, and Thomas, the usually stoic fisherman, wearing a wide, proud smile.

In that moment, as Lena looked out over the townspeople, the very fabric of her life, she felt more than just completeness. She felt expansion, like her heart had grown to encompass both the man beside her and the community before her.

The town had, in its own way, fallen for Alex just as she had. They saw in him what she did: a genuine soul with deep wells of kindness and stories that enriched their own narratives.

As she looked at Alex, she saw the echoes of her world reflected in his eyes. The man who had once known life mostly through the pages of books now had a vibrant, tangible chapter unfolding right here, in her town, beside her. And this chapter was as rich and textured as any he had ever penned.

His hand, warm and steady in hers, was more than just a physical touch. It was a symbol of their shared journey, a tactile reminder of their separate paths that had serendipitously merged into one. His touch spoke of a promise, a future crafted from both his world and hers, intertwined in ways neither could have envisioned, but now neither could imagine being without.

In the end, it wasn't just about Lena and Alex; it was about the joining of two worlds. The quiet, steadfast rhythm of the coastal town and the bustling, energetic pulse of Alex's city life were now harmonizing into a beautiful, shared melody.

And as Lena pressed her cheek to Alex's shoulder, she felt not the closing of a chapter, but the thrilling turn of a page into a new, shared journey that neither of them would have to walk alone.

Two Years Later

L ena and Alex's world was one brimming with profound love and shared purpose. Their coastal home, once Lena's solitary haven, now echoed with the joyful laughter and boundless curiosity of their little boy, Noah. Named after the timeless, calming rhythm of the sea that brought his parents together, Noah was a living testament to his parents' incredible journey, his bright eyes, a mesmerizing blend of Lena's deep blue and Alex's warm brown, reflecting the love story that was his origin.

Mornings in their home were a cherished ritual. Lena, whose soul was intertwined with the sun and the tides, would gently wake Noah. His soft coos were the family's new dawn, and together with Alex, they would greet the day as a united front.

Often, their mornings included a walk hand-in-hand to the lighthouse, where Noah's small, inquisitive face was lifted towards the vast sky, echoing his mother's lifelong connection with the sea and horizon.

In these moments, as Lena explained the purpose of the lighthouse and the ships it guided, Alex would marvel at the way his wife's eyes danced with the same light that had drawn him to her words. She was the woman who once existed beyond a screen, and here she was, his partner, his love, narrating the world to their son.

Alex, once a solitary writer who used his craft as a shield from the world, had transformed into a doting father. He found profound joy in reading stories to Noah, each word imbued with love and patience.

His voice, once reserved for crowded book readings, now danced intimately with every character he brought to life, teaching his son the magic that words could hold. Lena would watch them in these moments, her heart swelling in her chest, cherishing the man who had ventured out of his solitude to become the loving father sitting before her.

On weekends, the family would visit Mara's café, an integral part of their community routine. Here, under the inviting smell of fresh coffee and pastries, Noah would giggle at the foam mustache left on his lip from his steamed milk. His innocent mirth would ripple through the café, eliciting heartfelt smiles from the townspeople.

The community, initially skeptical, had wholeheartedly embraced Alex and the family he was building with Lena. They respected him, not for his acclaimed books, but for his genuine love for Lena and his dedication as a father to Noah.

In this café, where Lena once shared her first messages from Alex with Mara, the three of them sat as a family, secure, embraced, and home.

With Alex's latest novel inspired by his own life change and new-found love, Sam, his ever-supportive editor, saw not just the words on the page, but a friend who had found balance and peace. Sam marveled at how Alex's writing, once tinged with melancholy, now resonated with a deep and abiding warmth.

In Noah, Lena saw her connection to the town and the lighthouse deepening, while Alex saw the promise of fresh stories, a narrative shaped by love and family, extending far beyond what he had ever penned in his books. They were teaching Noah the beauty of a simple, purposeful life, a lesson they had learned from each other and the town that had become their shared haven.

Every evening, as they tucked Noah into bed under the soft, golden glow of his nightlight, Lena and Alex would exchange a knowing look that spoke volumes. In that family embrace was profound gratitude, love, and a little awe at the life they had built from a message in a bottle.

Alex would often press a gentle kiss to Lena's forehead, a simple but deep gesture, thanking her silently for the warmth she had brought into his life. She would lean into him, her stronghold, her partner in this remarkable journey, and draw strength from his presence just as she had from his words years ago.

Their nights would end with them side by side, reflecting on their day and dreaming about the ones to come. They would speak about the future, about Noah's growing curiosity, and about the lighthouse, which stood as both a literal and metaphorical beacon in their lives.

In these quiet moments, before sleep claimed them, Lena felt a profound sense of completeness. Their lives, once separated by miles and screens, were now as intertwined as the threads of the town's tapestry.

It was in this coastal haven that Lena and Alex were building not just a life, but a deeply rooted, expansive love story, with each other, and with this community that had opened its arms to them both.

In the calm of those nights, under the protective sweep of the lighthouse beam through their window, Lena and Alex found themselves not just in love, but in the love story they had both needed, sought, and finally found, nurturing their bond for whatever beautiful chapters lay ahead.

Milton Keynes UK
Ingram Content Group UK Ltd.
UKHW020935231123
433129UK00016B/743